Ju
F
B43   Bendet, Mayer.
          Shabbos treats that
       grew.

Ju
F
B43   Bendet, Mayer.
          Shabbos treats that
       grew.

Shabbos Treats That Grew

A Story by Mayer Bendet

Written by **Yaffa Leba Gottlieb**
Illustrated by **Miriam Lando**

Shabbos Treats That Grew

FIRST EDITION
First Impression — JUNE 1987

Published by
BASH PUBLICATIONS, INC.
5505 19th Avenue
Brooklyn, N.Y. 11204
(718) 236–8319

ISBN 0—932351—16—6 (Casebound Edition)
ISBN 0—932351—17—4 (Softcover Edition)
ISBN 0—932351—18—2 (Audio Cassette)

Distributed by:
MAZNAIM PUBLISHING CORPORATION
4304 12th Avenue
Brooklyn, New York 11219

Typography by BASH PUBLICATIONS, INC.
Printed in Singapore

One chilly Erev Shabbos afternoon, David Friedman and his younger sister Yehudis were on their way to Mr. Goldstein's grocery. They *thought* they were going there to do the Shabbos shopping for their mother, but you know how it is when you go to do a mitzvah, like shopping for Shabbos treats. You start with one mitzvah, and it leads to another, and to another until — well — you just never know how much a mitzvah will grow. David and Yehudis certainly didn't know. They were only thinking of helping their imma and also, of course, about buying their favorite treats in honor of Shabbos. . . .

"Potatoes, horseradish, cucumbers — here we are," said David as he began to fill the shopping cart with the groceries that were on his mother's list. "Yehudis, where are you going?"

"Here, David! Don't forget cookies! Vanilla sandwich cookies are my favorite!" called Yehudis, running ahead of her brother.

"Mine, too," David agreed. "But these have no hechsher, Yehudis. They aren't under the supervision of a rabbi. See, they don't have a mark on the label showing that they're kosher. Here's the brand that our imma always gets — *with* a hechsher."

And so, with the cookies safely in the cart, David and Yehudis continued to buy the best things in honor of Shabbos, until at the end of one aisle they suddenly stopped.

There they saw a little girl and her mother whom they had never seen before. What old and worn-out clothing they were wearing! Yes, they were also shopping for Shabbos. But they were not buying the best foods! The little girl's mother was looking at some dried-up vegetables, and she seemed to be wondering if she had enough money even for those!

"Come, David!" said Yehudis. "Let's wait in the checkout line behind that little girl and her mother and find out who they are!"

Yehudis smiled at the little girl. "Hi!" she introduced herself. "My name is Yehudis, and this is my brother, David. What's your name?"

"Chana," the little girl replied. "My mother and I just moved into a basement on Nettle Street this week, and I am so glad that it is almost Shabbos. My mother is buying groceries, and if we have enough money, she is going to buy some candy, too!" She showed Yehudis and David the package of candy she had picked out.

"*If* there's enough money?" Yehudis asked. She was sad that the girl was so poor. "Oh, I hope that there will be!"

But would there be? The children held their breath as Mr. Goldstein rang up the cash register. The purchases cost 83¢, 98¢, $1.29, $1.57 — number after number flashed before their eyes, until Mr. Goldstein rang up the total. "That's $15.34, Mrs. Schwartz," he said to Chana's mother.

Mrs. Schwartz opened her wallet and looked inside. "Oh, dear," she said, holding her money. "I have only fifteen dollars."

Mr. Goldstein didn't mind. "Don't worry," he said. "You can pay the rest the next time you come."

But Mrs. Schwartz looked worried. "No," she replied softly, shaking her head. "I don't want to owe anyone money. Chana, dear, please. Put back the candy."

Chana didn't say a word. She listened to her mother and returned the candy to the rack, just where it had been. "Oh, David! She's trying not to cry!" Yehudis whispered to her brother. "And her mother looks so sad!"

Poor Chana and her mother! They didn't want to take what they could not pay for, so Chana didn't have treats for Shabbos. And they had to live in a basement! That was all David and Yehudis could think of, all the way home.

"Imma! Guess what!" Yehudis cried as she and David hurried into the kitchen. "A little girl and her imma were so poor that they had to wear old, worn-out clothing, and they didn't even have enough money to buy candy for Shabbos!"

Her mother listened carefully to the children as they helped her put away the groceries. "Oh, dear!" she said when she had heard the whole story. "What can we do to help them?"

"We have to do *something*," David chimed in. "Boruch Hashem, we have so many Shabbos treats. Could we share ours with Chana?"

Imma smiled at David's excellent idea. "What a wonderful mitzvah that would be!" she agreed. "You bought treats for Shabbos, and now you want to share them with others. What a big mitzvah your treats are becoming!"

The children quickly filled a bag with in-honor-of-Shabbos treats, and hurried to Nettle Street, where Chana and her mother lived.

A chilly wind blew on the empty street as the children walked up and down, looking at the pleasant houses with their wide green lawns. "I wonder which one is Chana's," said David. Finally, a man came out of one of the houses.

"Can you help us, sir?" asked David politely. "Can you please tell us which house a little girl and her mother just moved into?"

"A little girl?" the man repeated. "A little girl with blond, curly hair? You must mean the little girl and her mother who moved into Mrs. Krupnik's basement. It's this house right over here." He was pointing behind them to a rickety old house that stood under the half-broken branches of an old tree. This house was different from the other houses on the block. The lawn was overgrown, the steps were broken, and the roof seemed to be falling apart.

The wind whistled shrilly through the tree's gray branches, and Yehudis's teeth began to chatter even though her coat was warm.

"David, I'm scared to go there!" she whispered to her brother.

"I-if Chana lives there, it can't be *so* bad," David insisted as he pushed open the creaking old gate. "Besides," he added, "Hashem protects people who go to do mitzvos."

The rickety porch steps wobbled and groaned as the children gently tiptoed up them. David took a deep breath and rang the doorbell. As soon as he touched it, a shrill bleat filled the air.

"David, let's *go!*" cried Yehudis, but she was too frightened to move. And then the old door creaked open.

"What do you children want?" An old gray-haired woman, with a scraggly cat clinging to her shoulder, appeared through the spider webs in the doorway. Holding her cane in her arm, she shook her bony finger at the children, shouting in a crackling voice, "Why are you bothering me?"

"Uh —" David began, "please excuse us, but do Chana Schwartz and her mother live here?"

"No, they don't," the old woman crackled. "They live in the basement! Go knock on the side door, and don't come back here!"

She slammed the door in their face.

David and Yehudis didn't have to be told twice. They hurried to the side door, and knocked as loudly as they could. No one answered. All they heard was the cawing of a lonely crow flapping through the gray autumn sky. "Chana!" called the children. "Are you here?"

At last Chana's mother came to the door, a frayed dish towel in her hands. "How nice of you to come and visit!" she greeted the children, welcoming them inside. "Please come in. I'll get Chana. She will be so happy to have company."

David and Yehudis stepped into the chilly little apartment. Although Mrs. Schwartz had swept it as clean as possible, it smelled damp and musty. Yehudis saw that there was a small kitchen on one side of the hallway, and a dim little living room, with two patched-up chairs, on the other side. Chana came out of the one small bedroom. Yes, these three dim, damp rooms were the whole apartment! How different from their own home, which was warm, cheery, and roomy!

"Hi!" said Chana, smiling shyly. The children could tell that she was glad they had come.

David said, "We, uh, well, uh, we wanted to welcome you to our neighborhood. We brought you some Shabbos treats. . . ."

"Oh!" exclaimed Chana. Her blue eyes sparkled and she clapped her hands with delight.

"How very thoughtful of you children!" Mrs. Schwartz said appreciatively. Her eyes looked misty behind her glasses, and she dabbed them with her dish towel. "Thank you so very much."

David felt a little uncomfortable at their gratefulness. "Well, uh, we're really glad you like them."

"Maybe Chana could come to our house and play," Yehudis suggested. "We still have a few hours before Shabbos, and my father could bring her home again on his way to shul."

"Could I go, Imma?" Chana asked. Her mother nodded in agreement, and what fun Yehudis and Chana soon had playing on the thick soft carpeting of Yehudis's living room. When it was time to wash and change for Shabbos, Chana took a Shabbos bath too, although she didn't have her Shabbos clothes with her.

"What fluffy towels you have!" Chana said happily. "And such nice warm water! We don't have much warm water in our basement."

"Oh, no!" thought Yehudis to herself. "Imagine living in that cold, damp basement, and not even being able to have a warm bath!"

Just then they heard Yehudis's mother calling, "Girls, are you ready? It's time to light the Shabbos candles!"

Chana and Yehudis hurried downstairs and watched as Yehudis's mother said the blessing over the Shabbos candles. How beautiful the candles looked in their shiny silver candlesticks, with their bright flames flickering. And how warm, clean, bright, and Shabbosdik the whole house was! Soon Yehudis's brother and father would come downstairs to go to shul . . . and . . . suddenly Chana burst into tears.

"Chana, what is the matter?" Yehudis's mother asked gently, as she put her arms around Chana to comfort her.

But Chana was crying and crying, until she finally said, through her sobs . . .

"My abba! He was so sick that he couldn't even stand up! Two men came and took him in an ambulance to the hospital. He had to have an operation, but now, boruch Hashem, he is getting better. With Hashem's help he will be home someday.

"We used to live in a nice house, like this one. But now we have so many doctors to pay that we had to sell our house and move into Mrs. Krupnik's basement. We'll probably have to stay there until my father is strong and healthy again."

When Yehudis and her family heard Chana's sad story, they felt like crying too. What could they do to help Chana and her mother?

And that is what David's and Yehudis's family thought about after they took Chana home that Shabbos. They sat together around their brightly lit Shabbos table, with steaming bowls of Shabbos chicken soup in front of them — yet somehow no one felt quite like eating, for they were thinking of Chana and her mother in that dreary, chilly basement. What could they do?... What could they do? . . . At last they thought of a plan!

On Sunday morning, David and Yehudis told the plan to their friends. "We'll make a grocery collection!" they announced. "We will ask our teachers to please help us organize it. Each week every child will bring some food for Chana and her mother, and we will deliver the bags of groceries to them on Friday afternoon. Maybe we will even be able to bring them enough food for the whole week! That will surely help them."

All the children and their teachers were eager to carry the plan out. With their parents' permission, each child volunteered to bring food for Chana — challahs, noodles, chicken, fish, fruits, vegetables, and, of course, Shabbos treats. "Our Shabbos treat mitzvah is *really* growing now," thought David as he collected the groceries at the end of the week and loaded them onto his wagon.

For two weeks the plan worked well, and David and Yehudis were able to deliver large bags of groceries to Chana and her mother, who received them gratefully. However, when they came on the third week with their wagon of groceries . . .

"David!" Yehudis whispered as they arrived at the old house. "Look! Mrs. Krupnik is standing in front of the gate! I think that she is not going to let us through!"

And indeed it appeared that she would not. "Why do you disturb me every week with your noisy wagon?" the old woman squawked at them in her crackly voice. "Go away!"

And David and Yehudis *felt* like running away — as quickly as they could. She was so mean! But they stopped themselves. Weren't their teachers and classmates depending on them to carry out this mitzvah? And what kind of Shabbos would Chana and her mother have if they couldn't have these Shabbos gifts? So Yehudis held tightly to the wagon handle and said bravely, "I'm sorry, Mrs. Krupnik, if we are disturbing you. But we just wanted to bring these packages to Chana and her mother."

"Hmmph!" said the old woman, shaking her head. "That's very nice! Chana and her mother moved in only a few weeks ago, and already you bring them packages! Well, I'm not letting you through! I've been living here for more than fifty years, and no one once brought a package for me!"

Yehudis looked at the angry old woman, her hand shaking as she held her cane, her cats meowing at her feet. Instead of being frightened, Yehudis suddenly felt sorry for her. Poor old woman! No one ever came to visit her? No one ever brought her a present?

"Please," she said to Mrs. Krupnik. "Take this bottle of grape juice, and this bag of oranges — for Shabbos!"

"Shabbos? Huh!" the old woman exclaimed. But she accepted the oranges and grape juice, and let the children through.

"You know what, David?" Yehudis whispered to her brother as they pulled their wagon up the walkway to Chana's basement door. "She probably really needs help. Maybe that's why she's always so angry."

"You're right, Yehudis," David agreed. "Next week, let's bring groceries for her along with the food we bring for Chana."

So that is what they did. The following week, they bravely knocked on the old woman's door, holding a full bag of groceries in their arms.

The old woman answered the door in her usual angry mood, but before she could say anything, Yehudis and David greeted her.

"Good Erev Shabbos, Mrs. Krupnik! We brought you a gift for Shabbos!"

The old woman threw up her hands in surprise, and even her cats gave a startled "Meow!" With shaking hands she took the groceries from the children, and she could hardly even speak to say thank you.

After the children left, Mrs. Krupnik went inside her old house, sat down on her rocking chair, and stared for a long, long time at the groceries, until tears began to well up in her eyes. The children had thought of her in her loneliness, and had even brought her a gift! "Well!" she finally said to herself. "Now I must do something, too!" She stood up from her rocker, took her cane, and did something that she had not done in many years — she went visiting.

Mrs. Schwartz was certainly surprised to see that Mrs. Krupnik had come to visit her. "My goodness!" thought Mrs. Schwartz. "What does Mrs. Krupnik want from us now?"

"Good afternoon," Mrs. Krupnik said politely. "Is it possible that I could come and spend Shabbos with you this evening?"

Mrs. Schwartz smiled. "Of course," she said. "That would be our pleasure. Please do come."

After a pleasant Shabbos meal, and after Chana had gone to sleep, Mrs. Schwartz and the elderly woman sat together in the dimly lit living room, sipping cups of hot tea. It was the first time that Mrs. Schwartz had ever seen Mrs. Krupnik smile.

"Tonight is the first time since my husband died, many years ago, that I have not spent Shabbos alone," said Mrs. Krupnik. "We always worked hard, yet we were quite poor, and although I wanted children badly, we didn't have any. After my husband died, I felt so sorry for myself, and so alone. But I didn't feel like being with people either, and children always bothered me, since I never had any of my own."

The old woman wiped away a tear. "Anyway," she continued, "I recently received a letter saying that my dear husband's uncle had died, leaving me all his money. Well, I didn't even know what to do with it! I put it in the bank — but it didn't make me happy.

"Yet when those children remembered me this afternoon, with their Shabbos gift — well, *that* was happiness! I even began to feel like being with people again, so I invited myself here for Shabbos. And I thank you, my dear, for accepting me here this evening! Now tell me about you!"

Mrs. Schwartz had been glad to listen to Mrs. Krupnik's story, but now she sighed as her thoughts turned to her own situation. She told how her husband had suddenly become ill, how he needed special doctors and nurses in the hospital day and night, and how it cost so much money that they had been forced to sell their house and nice things and move into the basement apartment where they now lived. "And everything is still so expensive," Mrs. Schwartz continued. "I'm sure Hashem will help us, but right now I just don't know what to do!"

"Aha!" Mrs. Krupnik exclaimed as she got up from her chair. "Well! *I* know *just* what to do! *I* will pay the doctor bills myself, *and* I'll fix up the upstairs of my house to make a nice home for you and Chana, and for your husband, may he soon have a speedy recovery! Then *you* won't have to worry, and *I* will have friends to keep me company!"

"And that's exactly what happened, Abba!" David told his father one evening at bedtime. "Mrs. Krupnik has made a nice upstairs apartment for Chana and her mother. When Chana's father heard about it, he began to feel better — and he should be home soon, too."

David's father smiled as he hugged his son good night. "We are really proud of you and Yehudis, son, for your share in this mitzvah."

David grinned. "Abba, it all grew out of one bag of Shabbos treats . . .

". . . but look how many people did mitzvos from it. We did a mitzvah by giving the treats to Chana. Then all our teachers and friends did mitzvos by organizing the grocery packages for Shabbos. Mrs. Krupnik did a mitzvah by helping Chana and her mother with the doctor bills and by making an apartment for them. And Chana and her mother did a mitzvah by keeping Mrs. Krupnik company! That's a lot of mitzvos growing from one bag of Shabbos treats, isn't it, Abba? Do you think it will grow any more?"

David's abba gave him a big hug and kissed him good night. "Grow more, David? Well . . . what do *you* think?"